PLEASE WASH
YOUR HANDS
BEFORE YOU READ ME
AND KEEP ME CLEAN

Max the Dragon

Peter Stern

Crown Publishers, Inc.
New York

for Charley and Katie

Copyright © 1990 by Peter Stern
All rights reserved. No part of this book may be reproduced or transmitted in any form or by any means, electronic
or mechanical, including photocopying, recording, or by any information storage and retrieval system, without
permission in writing from the publisher.
Published by Crown Publishers, Inc., a Random House company, 225 Park Avenue South, New York, New York 10003.
CROWN is a trademark of Crown Publishers, Inc.
Manufactured in the United States of America

Library of Congress Cataloging-in-Publication Data
Stern, Peter.
   Max the dragon / Peter Stern.
      p. cm.
   Summary: When the kings of Kloon order a dragon to
   get rid of the monster that plagues their land, tricksters
   send them an empty crate instead. But a dancing mouse
   stows away in the package and foils the monster with
   his graceful moves. [1. Monsters—Fiction. 2. Mice—Fiction.]
   I. Title. PZ7.S83894Max   1990   [E]—dc20   89–48310
   ISBN 0-517-57587-6 (trade)   CIP AC
         0-517-57588-4 (lib. bdg.)
First Edition
10 9 8 7 6 5 4 3 2 1

Once upon a time there was a grand old land called Kloon. It had sunshine and beaches, a nice breeze from the sea, and lots of hills. On top of each hill was a castle, because everyone who lived in Kloon was a king.

If it weren't for the monster, the place would have been perfect.

His name was Fragus, and he was a great stinking bully who strode around taking things that didn't belong to him. Gold, jewels–whatever gave a king a smile, Fragus stole.

Naturally, the kings were quite upset.

One midnight they held a secret meeting.
   "This has got to stop!" King Morgan began.
   "Absolutely," said King Bradley, nodding.
   "Simply can't go on," King Orip added.
   Then there was a pause.
   "What we must do…" Morgan went on.
   The kings leaned in. "Yes?"
   "…is get ourselves a…get ourselves a…"
   "Get ourselves a *what* exactly?" they asked.

"A...uh...a..." Morgan had no idea. Then, all of a sudden, he had: "A dragon!"

"Well, of course!" exclaimed Orip. The kings smiled. "A dragon—the very thing." And the search was on.

All through the night they pored over dragon literature until, finally, they came upon a catalog that offered a particularly dreadful-sounding one.

"That's him," they agreed. So they stacked up their gold and sent it off to the country that advertised dragons: Dilge.

At that time there weren't
many things in the world worse
than Fragus, but one of them was
Dilge. It was a purply-gray place,
full of belchy volcanoes, run by
three crooks named Crell, Crale,
and Crile. They lied about
everything.

"Great snake sale!" Crell would announce, holding up pieces of string. Or Crale would smack Crile on the back and say: "Hiya, Crale." Or Crile would try to sell pony rides on his alligator.

It was the same with the dragons. They didn't have any dragons. They'd never even seen one. They just pocketed the gold, sent back empty boxes, and laughed nastily at the great swindle of it.

Which is what they did when the gold from Kloon came. While a large crate stamped DRAGON was loaded onto a ship, these cheaters snorted and sniggered themselves silly.

And they missed something. Something important.

At the very instant the ship was pushed off, two fleet shapes dashed across the dock and jumped on board. Not until well out to sea did they stand up tall and straight in the midday sun—two remarkable figures: one a mouse, the other a bug. The mouse, a trim orangey fellow, was Max Parkinson, tap dancer. And the bug was his friend and adviser, Clement Farber. The two of them were off to seek their fortune anywhere the four winds blew. Because any place would be better than Dilge.

It's a long hard crossing from Dilge to Kloon, and the wind
whipped up the waves into great gray mountains. It cut
right through Max and Clement, making their teeth
click and chatter like dice. They badly needed
a cozy nook to curl up in. But when they
looked up and down the creaky deck,
all they saw was creaky deck.

And this box.

They moved closer, to read the printing on it.
"Oh boy!" exclaimed Max, turning back. Clement stuck
out his hand and stopped him. "We've gotta get in."

"With dragons?"

"Here's the way it is, Max," Clement
explained. "Get in or freeze."

Clement had a way of cutting a
problem down to size. So, as quietly
as they could, the two of them slipped inside.

No dragon!

"Yay!" They snuggled up in a corner, shared a carrot, and talked about their hopes. Max wanted theaters to dance in and lots of applause. Clement wanted to be rich as a king. With these happy thoughts tumbling around in their heads, the two pals fell asleep.

Hard months of travel brought the ship nearer and nearer Kloon, until one sunny April morning it was there.

Orip saw it first. "The dragon's here!" he bellowed. All over Kloon, kings tumbled out of their castles, ran down their hills, and tripped over each other racing to see it.

Their eyes gleamed at the sight, as Morgan had the box very carefully unloaded. Then he stepped forward and unsnapped the latch. The door began to open. The kings gasped.

There, strutting out to greet them, was this tiny little thing.

"S-smallish sort of a one," whispered Morgan.

"Mmmmmmm. Bit on the skimpy side," agreed Bradley.

"Doesn't appear to be…er…" Orip hesitated. "…quite the model we specified."

"Hi!" said Max, smiling. "Where exactly is this?"

"Mr. D-dragon," Morgan stammered, "this is Kloon." He'd never spoken to a dragon before and wasn't sure when the fire came out. "My name is King Morgan, and these are the other kings. We're all kings here."

Clement liked the sound of the place at once.

"We've sent for you to take care of Fragus," explained Bradley.

"Uh huh," said Max, nodding.

"What's Fragus?" asked Clement.

"He's this big—" "He's that terrible—" All the kings spoke at once. Max got the idea.

"And if I…uh…took care of him, would I be able to stay on here?"

"Of course," replied Orip. "You could move right into his place." He pointed to the biggest castle on the highest hill.

Clement buzzed in. "We'd need a theater, too."

"Whatever for?" asked Morgan.

"To dance in, of course."

"Oh," said the kings. "Absolutely."

Clement smiled. "Good. It's a deal."

Suddenly the earth shook with a *B'DDUM B'DDUM* rumbling. The kings started trembling like wobbly teacups. A cloud of red dust was approaching. Horrible screams trumpeted ahead: "YUGG! YUGG!"

"That'll be…uh…him now," said Morgan. "We'd best be off." The kings dashed over to the woods.

Max turned. And there was
Fragus. What a sight! He was
enormous, ugly, and filthy, with
broken yellow teeth and lots of glassy
eyes. And a smell! Everywhere he
went the flowers died.

"Let's get out of here," Max yelled.

"Hold it." Clement stopped him.

"What?"

"You've gotta stay and fight this bum."

"Are you kidding?"

"We just promised the kings."

"But..." But Max knew Clement was right, so he
turned back to Fragus, held up his stick, and shouted in
the most menacing voice he could manage:

"STOP!"

Fragus, however, wasn't stopping. Closer and closer he thundered, turning everything into a jumble of dust and noise and smell. Max shut his eyes and braced himself for the crash.
B'DDUM B'DDUM B'DDUM

No crash. Max opened his eyes. No Fragus. The monster had charged right by. He hadn't even seen the mouse.

The kings raced over from the woods.

"That was him," shouted Morgan.

"Weren't you going to burn him to a crisp or something?" asked Bradley.

"I wanted to…er…look him over first," Max explained.

"Oh." The kings nodded. "How sensible."

"It's the way he works," Clement told them. "First the looking the job over, then…"

B'DDUM B'DDUM B'DDUM

In a flash the kings were back in the woods.

"Now what?" Max yelled to Clement.

"Well, you've got to get his attention. That's the first thing."

Max nodded and darted up the side of the crate to where Fragus could see him.

"Now dance," Clement called. "Give him the old razzle-dazzle."

Max danced. He jumped right into the act he'd done clear across Dilge. He tippy-tapped this way, then kicked out that way, then whirled gracefully this way, then tapped some more.

The kings clapped.

Fragus stopped.

"WHAT IS YOU?" he roared.

Dum Da Dee Da Dum. A full orchestra was playing in Max's head. *Tippy tappy tip* here. *Tappy tip tap* there.

"WHAT IS YOU?" Fragus roared again.

Max froze. His lips locked. "GRLZFERRRRPN," came out.

"EH?" asked Fragus.

"YRFLOOPNZ," Max said.

"HUH?"

"BRKLEEPYS!" screamed Max.

Fragus tried one more time. "WHAT IS YOU?" he bellowed. It's amazing Max wasn't knocked right off. The breath smell alone could have done it.

But the mouse had found his voice.

He swelled his chest and boomed out, loud and clear:
"I am MAX. MAX THE DRAGON!" It echoed all over.
"MAX-AX-AX the DRAGON-AGON-AGON!"

Clement clapped.

The kings cheered.

Max bowed.

SMUNCH! A huge claw came crashing down on the crate.
Clement yelled, "No bowing, Max. Dance. For your life!"

Max leaped and twisted and twirled like never before.
He tapped and kicked his heels over here—as a claw came
whamming down there. Then he glided and turned and
twisted around there—as a claw came smashing down here.

Fragus was astonished. All his eyes were wide open and staring in more or less the same direction: at this fabulous Little Dancing Thing. Clearly the kings prized it. They were clapping. And if they liked it so much, he had to have it, whatever it was. But every time he reached out to grab, it neatly sidestepped and pirouetted out of reach. When he lunged, it leaped. When he grasped, it spun away like a top.

"Go, dragon!" shouted the kings, who'd never seen such fine footwork.

YUGG!

The monster flung his whole smelly self at the wonderful thing, and this time Max grand-jetéd right off the top of the crate. He whirled gracefully down through the air, in the fifth position, and landed on point.

Then he tapped on into the box.

CLACKETY CLACKETY CLICK CLICK. The sounds of Max's tapping reverberated as if he were dancing in a great hall. He could almost picture row upon row of cheering people, yelling and waving at him. He felt wonderful, as though he could do anything.

For his part, Fragus had never wanted anything so much in his life. He hurled himself into the box. Max deftly swooped up one wall, timestepped across the ceiling, and bounced outside.

At that exact moment Clement buzzed over like lightning, put his shoulder to the door, and heaved until it swung—

KERCHUNK–shut.

"HIP, HIP…" From the woods a cheer went up, and a hundred crowns were tossed in the air.

"HOORAY FOR THE DRAGON!" The kings raced
over. Max took a bow. Clement beamed. King Morgan
said, in a firm and happy voice, "Mr. Dragon—"

"Call me Max."

"Max, you've done it. Thank you. Fragus's castle is
yours, and we hope you'll stay here forever."

Max looked at the kindly kings and at Kloon shining in
the setting sun—his dreams were starting to come true.
He winked over at Clement and, just at that very second,
had one of his best ideas ever. He grinned a spectacular grin.

He and Clement had the kings reload the box onto the ship, and sent it off–back to Dilge. What a perfect surprise for Crell, Crale, and Crile!

That's how the good times came to Kloon, and stayed. Nobody ever got too gloomy from then on, because however bad things seemed, a guy could always go and catch a show at Max the Dragon's Place.

KERCHUNK–shut.

"HIP, HIP…" From the woods
a cheer went up, and a hundred
crowns were tossed in the air.

"HOORAY FOR THE DRAGON!" The kings raced
over. Max took a bow. Clement beamed. King Morgan
said, in a firm and happy voice, "Mr. Dragon—"

"Call me Max."

"Max, you've done it. Thank you. Fragus's castle is
yours, and we hope you'll stay here forever."

Max looked at the kindly kings and at Kloon shining in
the setting sun—his dreams were starting to come true.
He winked over at Clement and, just at that very second,
had one of his best ideas ever. He grinned a spectacular grin.